so many gifts

a story by Anne Marie Pierce

Anne Marie Pierce 1996

FORWORD
p.o. box 533
Crookston, Minnesota 56716

ISBN   0-9623937-0-3

u. i. o. g. d.

to my father who fostered my creativity.
to my mother who gives me the courage to use it.
I am fortunate to love them both.

so many gifts

it was a very long time ago,
in a place I can't remember.

almost like magic,
there was a man.

he was different. not peculiar really, just unusual.

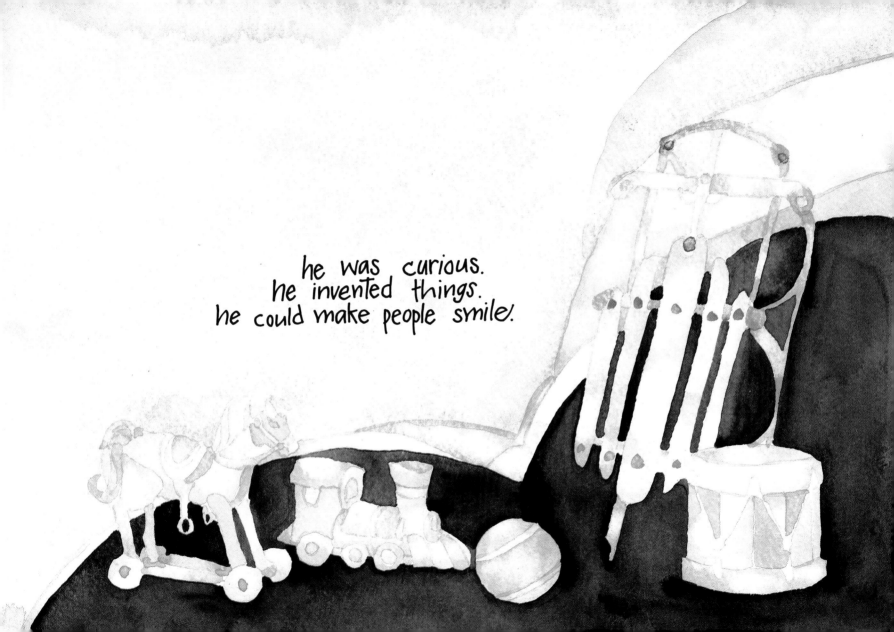

he was curious.
he invented things.
he could make people smile!

he called himself Santa.
no one asked why.
it was a kindly name as was the man.
people liked him,
and he liked them back.

Santa especially enjoyed the children.
he watched them play.
he studied their faces.

there he saw honesty and trust.
he sensed their curiosity.
like him, their joy was discovery.

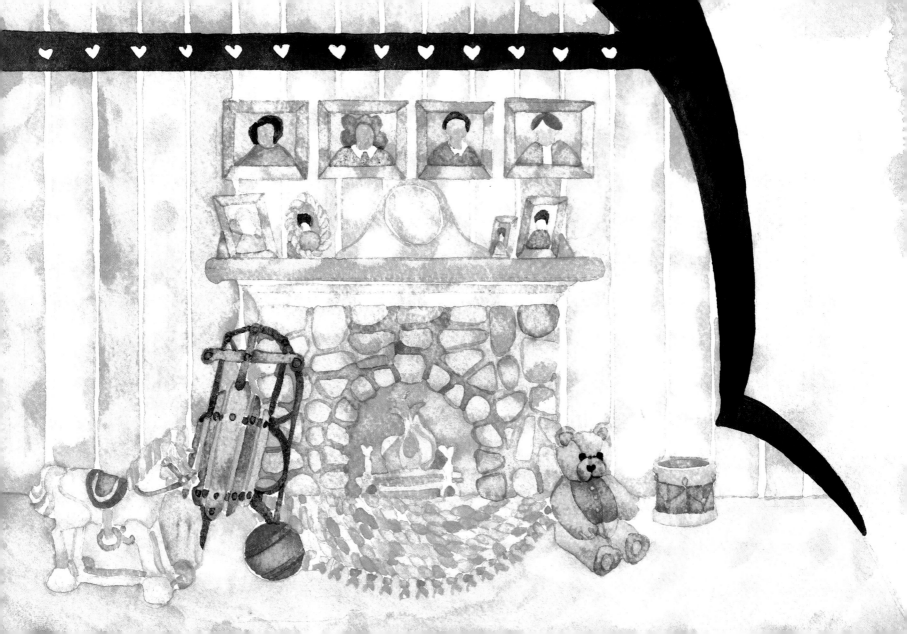

Santa made them special games.
he captured their attention.

his ideas were fun,
but the challenge was real.

how he loved them!
their laughter was his reward.

slowly, he reached a decision.
the children would be his work.
his tool, imagination.
his classroom, the earth.
his dream, that all would be gifted.

he had many ideas.
he worked for hours.
his joy was endless.

each day, the children played around him.
he loved their company, but he was distracted.

every minute, every hour was so important.
he soon realized he must be alone.

only dedication would fulfill the dream.
so Santa went away.

he left with a promise:
once a year, he would return to the children.

he'd travel at night bringing each a gift.
a special gift.
a wondrous gift full of ideas.
a gift of imagination.

word spread. the excitement grew.
soon there were new places,
and many children looking for Santa.

too many stops for just one man.

there had to be helpers.
but who, and where could they be?

then, he remembered.
the grown children.
those he had visited before.

could they share the gifts with others?

he found many eager to learn.

they worked quickly
so all children could know the dream.

with Santa,
they developed
endless supplies of fantasy and myth.

years have passed.
the plan is unchanged.

Santa visits the youngest children,
planting seeds of discovery.

later, his assistants see that the magic continues.

in time, children grow
to become helpers and the cycle repeats.

there have been so many gifts.

there is wonder and delight.
mystery and challenge.

a world of dreams for everyone!